KU-213-268

Schools Library and Information Services
S00000649092

Kiss, Kiss!

PUBLIC LIBRARY

L -46653

649092 | SCH

JYWIL

Margaret Wild & Bridget Strevens-Marzo

LITTLE HARE

One day, when Baby Hippo woke up,
he was in such a rush to go and play that he
forgot to give his *mum* a kiss.

"Aw!" said Mum.

Through the squelchy, squelchy mud waddled Baby Hippo.
And this is what he heard...

"Kiss, kiss!"

Around the bumpy, bumpy rocks waddled Baby Hippo.
And this is what he heard...

"Kiss, kiss!"

Up the mossy, mossy bank waddled Baby Hippo.

And this is what he heard...

"Kiss, kiss!"

Through the long, long grass waddled Baby Hippo.
And this is what he heard...

"Kiss, kiss!"

Under the leafy, leafy trees waddled Baby Hippo.
And this is what he heard...

"Kiss, kiss!"

Baby Hippo stopped. He suddenly remembered
something he'd forgotten to do.

Baby Hippo hurried back under the leafy, leafy trees,

through the long, long grass,

down the mossy, mossy bank,

around the bumpy, bumpy rocks,

through the squelchy, squelchy mud, to find his mum.

But he couldn't see his *mum* anywhere.
"Aw!" said Baby Hippo.

Then out of the deep, deep water appeared two eyes,
two wiggling ears and a pair of snorting nostrils.
"Peekaboo!" said Mum.

Baby Hippo beamed.
"Kiss, kiss?" he said.
"Kiss, *kiss!*" said Mum.

For Karen and Olivia—MW

For Ella—BS-M

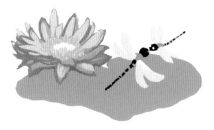

Little Hare Books
4/21 Mary Street, Surry Hills
NSW 2010 AUSTRALIA

Copyright © text Margaret Wild 2003
Copyright © illustrations Bridget Strevens-Marzo 2003

First published 2003

All rights reserved. No part of this publication may be reproduced, stored in a retrieval system or transmitted in any form or by any means, electronic, mechanical, photocopying, recording or otherwise, without the prior written permission of the publisher.

National Library of Australia
Cataloguing-in-Publication entry
    Wild, Margaret, 1948-.
    Kiss, kiss!

    ISBN 1 877003 14 X.

    1. Farewells – Juvenile fiction. 2. Jungle animals – Juvenile
    fiction. I. Strevens-Marzo, Bridget. II. Title.

    A823.3

Designed by ANTART
Produced by Phoenix Offset
Printed in Hong Kong

5 4 3 2 1